Pinocchio and the Great Whale

By Carlo Collodi

Adapted by David E. Cutts

Illustrated by Diane Paterson

TROLL ASSOCIATES

Library of Congress Cataloging in Publication Data

Cutts, David.
    Pinocchio and the great whale.

    (The Adventures of Pinocchio library; 4)
    Summary: Pinocchio saves his father and himself
when they rediscover each other in the stomach of a
great whale, and then shows his good heart by toiling
away in order to care for his sick father and the Fairy.
    [1. Puppets and puppet plays—Fiction.   2. Fairy
tales]   I. Collodi, Carlo, 1826-1890.   II. Paterson,
Diane, 1946-   ill.   III. Title.   IV. Series.
PZ8.C96Pg   [Fic]   81-16026
ISBN 0-89375-720-9   AACR2
ISBN 0-89375-721-7 (pbk.)

Printed in the United States of America
10 9 8 7 6 5 4 3 2 1

Pinocchio had been good all year, so his friend the Good Fairy said, "Tomorrow you shall stop being a puppet, and become a real boy. We will hold a special breakfast celebration in your honor." As Pinocchio left to invite his friends to the celebration, the Fairy called out, "Take care, Pinocchio. Remember to return home before dark." And the puppet promised to return in an hour.

3

In less than an hour, Pinocchio had invited all his friends. He found Candlewick, the laziest and naughtiest of his friends, hiding on someone's porch. Candlewick said, "I am waiting for the midnight coach, which will take me to the Land of Donkeys. It is a wonderful place where there are no schools, and everyone plays all day long. Why don't you come, too?"

"Oh, no," said Pinocchio. "I promised to be home before dark. But tell me, are you going alone?" Candlewick explained that more than a hundred boys would be riding in the coach. "That would be a great sight to see, but I must go home," said Pinocchio. "Wait two minutes longer," said Candlewick. And before Pinocchio realized it, those two minutes had stretched into two hours.

"Are you sure there is never any school in the Land of Donkeys?" asked Pinocchio. "Never!" replied Candlewick. "It sounds like a delightful place," sighed Pinocchio. "Then come with me," coaxed his friend. But Pinocchio replied, "Oh, I really can't." At that very moment, the midnight coach came down the road. "Here it comes!" cried Candlewick.

The coach was pulled by twelve pairs of donkeys with boots on their feet. The coachman was so jolly that dozens of boys had already squeezed into the coach just to ride with him. Candlewick quickly climbed aboard. "Come with us and have fun," he called to Pinocchio. "Yes," called all the boys. "Come with us and have fun!" And finally Pinocchio said, "Make room for me!"

There was no more room in the coach, so Pinocchio had to ride on one of the donkeys. As he rode along, he heard the donkey whispering. It seemed to say, "Boys who turn their backs on school come to a bad end. I know this from experience." Then a tear ran down the donkey's cheek. "Don't pay attention to that stupid beast," laughed the coachman, snapping his whip.

By daybreak, they had arrived in the Land of Donkeys. What a wonderful place it was! Boys were everywhere, playing ball, riding bikes, chasing one another, walking on their hands, and generally having fun. As soon as the coach stopped, Pinocchio, Candlewick, and the others joined right in.

The hours became days, and the days stretched into weeks. Whenever Pinocchio saw Candlewick, he said, "You were right, my friend! And to think that I almost missed out on all this fun!" For five months, there was nothing but fun and games. But one morning, when Pinocchio awoke, he had quite a surprise.

During the night, his ears had turned into a perfect pair of donkey ears! Pinocchio ran to find Candlewick. Imagine his surprise when he discovered that his friend had also caught "donkey fever." Before long, their hands became hoofs, and their faces turned into donkey muzzles. They even grew donkey tails!

In less than two hours, they looked exactly like donkeys in every way. And when they tried to talk, they could only bray. All play and no study had turned them into perfect donkeys. Before long, the coachman took them away and sold them in the market, for that was how he made his living. Poor Pinocchio! He was sold to a man who needed a donkey to dance in his circus.

For three months, Pinocchio practiced jumping through hoops
and dancing on his hind legs. Then he was made the star of the
circus, and people came from far and near just to see the
famous dancing donkey. Unfortunately, Pinocchio tripped
while jumping through a hoop, and hurt his leg. The doctor
said that he would be lame for life.

Pinocchio was sent to market, but no one would buy him.
After all, what good is a lame donkey? Finally, a man came
along who wanted to make a drum. "This donkey's skin is nice
and thick," he said. "It would make a good strong drum." So
he bought the lame donkey. Imagine how Pinocchio felt now!
He didn't want to be made into a drum!

When the man had paid for Pinocchio, he took him to the seashore. He found a heavy stone and tied it to the donkey's neck. Then he tied a long rope to one of Pinocchio's hind legs, and pushed him into the water. The stone was so heavy that Pinocchio sank down, down, down. And then a remarkable thing happened.

When the man thought his lame donkey had been drowned, he pulled the rope in. But instead of a donkey, he found a wooden puppet! You see, the Fairy had turned Pinocchio from a donkey back into a puppet again. "Oh well," said the man. "At least I can sell the puppet for firewood." But Pinocchio broke away, and jumped back into the water.

He was glad that he was no longer a donkey. So he swam and he swam, far out to sea. Suddenly, he saw something coming toward him. It was the gigantic head of a terrible sea monster. Its jaws were open wide, and Pinocchio could see row after row of sharp, pointed teeth. It was the great whale!

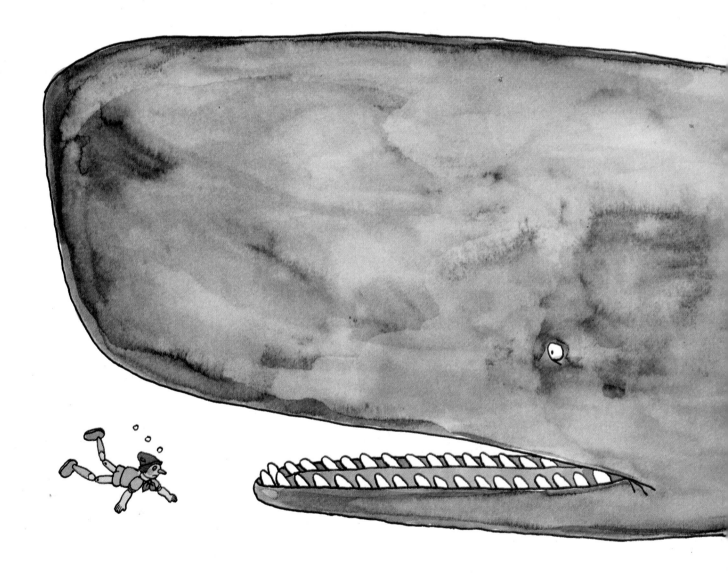

Pinocchio tried to swim the other way, but it was too late. He was sucked into the gigantic mouth with such force that he was knocked unconscious. When he woke up, it was so dark that he could hardly see. Then he realized that he was inside the stomach of the great whale. He began at once to cry for help.

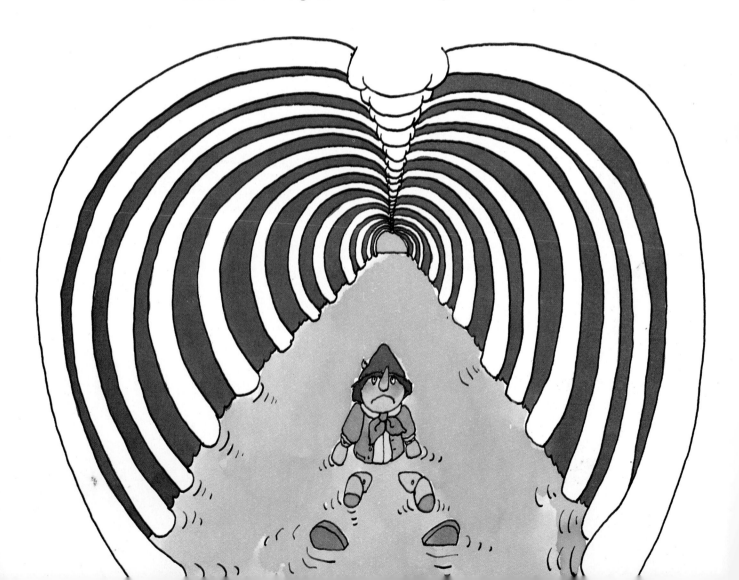

"No one can help you now," said a nearby voice. It was a tuna who had been swallowed at the same time as Pinocchio. "Just relax and wait for the great whale to digest you," said the tuna. But Pinocchio cried, "I don't want to be digested. I want to escape." Suddenly, he saw a faint light in the distance. "What's that?" he asked. But the tuna did not know.

As Pinocchio made his way toward the light, he saw that it was a candle. It was sticking out of a bottle that was sitting on a table. An old man sat near the table. When Pinocchio got closer, he saw that the man was Geppetto. "Father!" cried Pinocchio. "Pinocchio!" cried the old man. And they hugged each other until their arms ached. Of course, Pinocchio told him everything that had happened.

Then Geppetto explained how he had survived in the whale's stomach. "When the whale swallowed me, he also swallowed a merchant ship that was loaded with supplies," he said. "I found tins of meat, cheese, and raisins to eat. But now they are gone, and this is the last candle." Pinocchio said, "We must escape." Geppetto asked, "But how? And when?"

"When the whale falls asleep, we will escape," said Pinocchio.
So that night, when the great whale slept, Pinocchio and
Geppetto climbed up his throat and tiptoed across his tongue.
Then they jumped out of his huge mouth and into the sea.
Geppetto did not know how to swim, so Pinocchio held him on
his shoulders as he swam toward the distant shore.

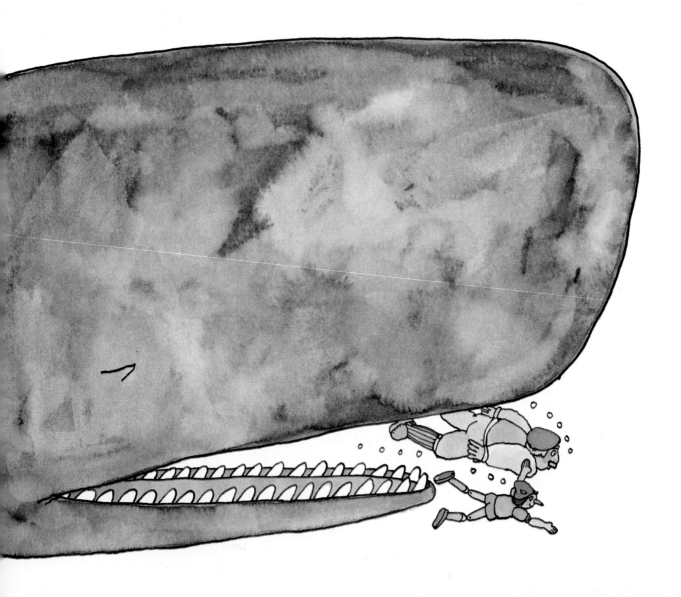

Pinocchio was a good swimmer, but the shore was far away. He swam and he swam until his strength began to fail, and he had no breath left. When he knew he could go no farther, he cried, "Help me! I am drowning." A moment later, father and son heard a voice call out, "I will help you."

It was the same tuna that Pinocchio had met inside the whale. "How did you escape?" asked Pinocchio. "I simply followed your good example," replied the tuna. "Now climb up on me, and I will bring you safely to the beach." So Pinocchio and Geppetto climbed up onto his back and were given a comfortable ride to shore.

Soon the puppet and his father had their feet on dry land again. They thanked the tuna for his help and waved good-by. Since morning had come, they set off down the road, looking for a house where they might find some breakfast. Geppetto was so weak that he had to lean on his son to keep from falling down.

They came to a little straw hut. Inside it was the Talking Cricket. "Oh, my dear little friend," cried Pinocchio. But the Cricket scolded, "Now you call me 'friend,' but long ago, you chased me from your house." Sadly, Pinocchio said, "Then you should chase me now." But instead, the Cricket made a soft bed for Geppetto and sent the puppet out to fetch him a glass of warm milk.

A farmer at a nearby farm made Pinocchio work for the glass of milk. The puppet worked as hard as a donkey. Even when he was exhausted, he kept working. Then the farmer gave him the milk. "I once had a donkey, but he died. His name was Candlewick," said the farmer. "Oh, no," thought Pinocchio. "Poor Candlewick."

For the next five months, Pinocchio returned each morning to the farm. He worked all day for milk and eggs for his sick father. In the evenings, he learned to weave baskets, which he sold at the market. He even made a wheelchair for Geppetto. By working long and hard, he managed to care for his father, and save a little money besides.

One day, as Pinocchio was going into town, he saw a snail. She was the same snail who kept house for the Good Fairy. "The Fairy is sick and dying," said the snail. "She cannot afford to buy food or medicine." At once, Pinocchio gave her all the money he had, saying, "If you return in two days, I will have more money for the Fairy."

29

Then Pinocchio went straight home and set to work. He knew that it would be hard to care for both his father and the Fairy. But he would willingly work longer hours and weave more baskets to sell. That night, instead of weaving only eight baskets, he stayed up late, and made sixteen. It was after midnight when he finally fell asleep.

While he slept, he had a dream. In his dream, the Fairy appeared and said, "Well done, Pinocchio! People who care for others deserve praise and love. To reward you for your good heart, I forgive you for everything that has happened in the past. In the future, if you simply do the best you can, you will find happiness." Then the dream ended.

When Pinocchio awoke, he looked around him. The house was no longer a straw hut. Geppetto was no longer in his wheelchair. And best of all, Pinocchio was no longer a wooden puppet. At last he had become a real boy! He walked over and looked at an old puppet hanging in the corner. Then he laughed merrily, and said, "How foolish I was when I was just a wooden puppet!" He was so happy now that he was a real boy.